For Peter and Sally, with love — T.C.

For Lorenzo — S.M.

First published 2017 by Nosy Crow Ltd
The Crow's Nest, 14 Baden Place, Crosby Row, London SE1 1YW
www.nosycrow.com

ISBN 978 1 78800 075 8

Nosy Crow and associated logos are trademarks
and/or registered trademarks of Nosy Crow Ltd

Text © Tracey Corderoy 2017
Illustrations © Sarah Massini 2017

The right of Tracey Corderoy to be identified as the author
and Sarah Massini to be identified as the illustrator of this work has been asserted.

A CIP catalogue record for this book is available from the British Library.

Printed in Turkey
Papers used by Nosy Crow are made from wood grown in sustainable forests.

1 3 5 7 9 8 6 4 2

The
Boy
and
the
Bear

Tracey Corderoy
& Sarah Massini

nosy crow

Once upon a time,
there lived a boy
who wanted to play.

But all the best games . . .

like see-saw . . .

and catch . . .

and hide-and-seek
needed two.

And the boy was all alone.

There was Bear, of course.

But Bear was just a bear.

Not a boy who wanted to play.

Besides, Bear was shy.

Too shy even to stop and say hello.

Then, one summer morning,
as the boy sat alone, a paper boat
bobbed across the water.

On the boat was a message.
It said,

BOO!

"But who would say boo?"
wondered the boy.
"Oh! A Best Friend would
say boo, that's who!"

He quickly wrote back —

— and he sailed his boat across the water.

Then what should come back

but another boat.

Yes!

— wrote the boy —

Wh en?

He waited

and waited.

Then —

NOW!

— came the reply.

And out peeped . . .

. . . Bear!

"Oh, it's just you," sighed the boy.
"I thought it might be a Best Friend."

Bear hung his head,
and turned to go.

"Wait!" called the boy. "Come back! Would you like to play hide-and-seek?"

With an eager nod, Bear tiptoed off to hide, and the boy started to count.

"Ready or not!" he shouted. "I'm coming!"

But Bear
didn't understand
hide-and-seek.

And he was too heavy for see-saw.

The next day,
they tried catch.

But that didn't
work either.

Bear couldn't play the boy's games.

"Never mind," sighed the boy.

"We'll just have to think of something else."

Then, one autumn morning,
Bear **did** think of something.

He started to build . . .

. . . a treehouse!

"Good idea!" said the boy.
"Can I help?"

He passed Bear the logs,

      and Bear tied them in place.

Bear knew exactly what to do.

And at last they finished the treehouse, together.

There was a window to gaze out of
at the moon, and a chair
big enough for two.

"Oh, Bear!"
the boy smiled.
"Look what we've made!
It's perfect!"

They stayed in their treehouse
until the leaves
tumbled down . . .

and the first snowflakes fell.

Then, one winter morning,
the boy found a small frosty boat
on the pond.

MUST GO.

"No!" the boy cried.

"Bear!

Bear!"

But there was no Bear
anywhere.

The boy thought of his friend
through the long chilly days . . .

and the dark starry nights.

He waited all through winter.

Bear?

Where are you?

Are you asleep?

But the boy's words froze solid
on the icy pond.

Winter passed and spring came.
Then one morning, as the sun rose,
the boy saw three boats bobbing on the water.

I'M AWAKE!

I MISSED YOU...

ARE YOU THERE?

"Yes! I'm here!"
shouted the boy.
"But where are you?"

And out of the trees . . .

came the boy's Best Friend . . .

. . . Bear.